Paige
the Pantomime
Fairy

For Zoë Sarankin, a very good
friend of the fairies

 Special thanks to
Narinder Dhami

ORCHARD BOOKS
338 Euston Road, London NW1 3BH
Orchard Books Australia
Level 17/207 Kent Street, Sydney, NSW 2000
A Paperback Original

First published in 2006 by Orchard Books

A CIP catalogue record for this book is available
from the British Library.

ISBN 978 1 84616 209 1
1 3 5 7 9 10 8 6 4 2

Printed and bound in China

Orchard Books is a division of Hachette Children's Books,
an Hachette Livre UK company.

www.hachettelivre.co.uk

Paige

the Pantomime
Fairy

by Daisy Meadows

illustrated by Georgie Ripper

ORCHARD

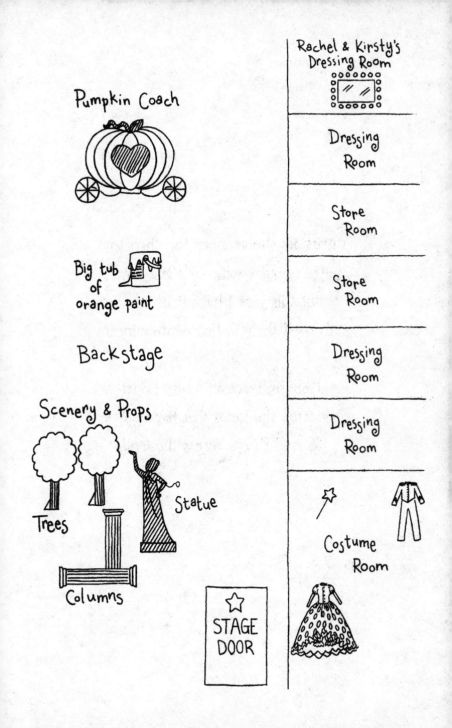

Christmas shows more fun than toys
Are popular with girls and boys,
But this year I have it in mind
To spoil their festive pantomimes.

Goblins, leave this very hour!
Bring me the items that have power
To ruin shows across the land,

Ballet slipper
slip-up

Contents

Casting Crisis

"Only three more days until Christmas!" Rachel Walker said, skipping down Tippington High Street and beaming happily at her best friend Kirsty Tate. "I'm so glad you could come and stay, Kirsty, even if it is just for a few days."

"Me too," Kirsty Tate agreed, looking excited. She had arrived the day before, and her parents were coming to Tippington to pick her up again on Christmas Eve. "I hope it snows, don't you? It makes Christmas so magical."

"And magic is something we know all about!" Rachel laughed. Kirsty grinned. She knew exactly what Rachel meant. Ever since the two girls had met on a magical holiday to Rainspell Island, they had become best friends with the fairies.

"One, two, three!" Rachel counted as she practised her dance steps along the pavement. "This is the trickiest step in my dance for the Christmas Show. I want it to be perfect."

Rachel was dancing in the Tippington Christmas pantomime, which this year was a performance of Cinderella. On Christmas Eve, Rachel would be one of four girls dancing in the ballroom scene.

Rachel and Kirsty were on their way to Tippington Theatre, for a rehearsal.

"Thanks for inviting me to the rehearsal," Kirsty said happily as they reached the theatre. "I wish I could come to the actual performance."

"Me, too." Rachel agreed, looking glum. "But the tickets sold out really fast. I couldn't even get any for my mum and dad!" Then she brightened. We're practising the ballroom scene today, though, so at least you'll see my dance."

The girls went in through the stage door. There was a lot of hustle and bustle backstage, and Kirsty looked round with interest.

"Rachel! Kirsty!" a girl's voice called.

The girls turned and saw Karen Lewis, a friend of Rachel's from school, waving at them and looking really excited.

"Karen is one of the dancers in the ballroom scene too," Rachel told Kirsty, as Karen came rushing over.

"Rachel, our costumes have arrived!" Karen said with a big smile.

"Oh!" Rachel looked thrilled. "I thought they weren't coming until the final rehearsal tomorrow."

"Well, they're here!" laughed Karen. "I can't wait to see what we're wearing."

The three girls hurried to the backstage room where the costumes had been laid out. Most of the cast members were there already, and there was a buzz of excited chatter.

Rachel glanced round the room at the colourful costumes which all had labels pinned to them.

"Ours are over here!" called Karen from the other side of the room.

Rachel and Kirsty hurried to look.
A beautiful white full-length ballet dress
with underskirts of crisp white net lay
on a chair. It was labelled 'Rachel
Walker'. Beside the dress lay a pair of
pink satin ballet shoes with long satin
ribbons and a pink rose for Rachel to
wear in her hair. All four dancers had
the same costume.

"Oh, it's beautiful!" Kirsty breathed.

"I can't wait to try it on," said Rachel, holding the dress carefully against her.

Just then a short man carrying a clipboard came into the room, looking very worried. "Karen, Rachel, please go and change into your costumes right away," he said, mopping his brow with a spotted handkerchief. "I'm afraid we've got all sorts of problems. Nobody's costume fits properly and the wardrobe mistress doesn't think she's going to have time to alter them all. We need to know if your costumes fit you."

"Yes, Mr Robinson," said Rachel. Kirsty remembered Rachel telling her that he was the director of the show.

"Mr Robinson!" a stagehand cried, rushing into the room looking flustered. "Clarissa Murray's mum has just phoned. Clarissa's got chicken-pox. She can't dance in the show!"

"What?" Mr Robinson groaned. "Oh, no!"

"What a shame!" Kirsty said.
"Poor Clarissa."

Mr Robinson was pacing anxiously
up and down. "The dance won't work
with just three girls," he was muttering.
"We must have four. Oh, this is
a disaster!"

Kirsty and Rachel glanced at each other, and Kirsty knew that they were both thinking the same thing.

"Maybe I could take Clarissa's place!" Kirsty suggested breathlessly.

Paige Appears

Mr Robinson turned to her. "And who are you, my dear?" he asked.

"Kirsty Tate," replied Kirsty. "I'm Rachel's friend, and I'm staying with her until Christmas Eve."

"I can teach Kirsty the steps," Rachel added quickly.

"And I'll practise every single minute

until the show!" said Kirsty.

"Well, that solves our problem!" Mr Robinson said, looking delighted. "Thank you very much!" He glanced at Kirsty. "You look about the same size as Clarissa. Why don't you try her costume and see if it fits?" And then he hurried off.

"Isn't this brilliant?" Rachel said with a beaming smile. "Now you're going to be in the show too!"

Kirsty grinned. "I just hope I can learn the steps in time," she said.

They found the dress labelled 'Clarissa
Murray' and Kirsty picked it up. The
rose for her hair lay next to it but, to
Kirsty's dismay, there was only one pink
ballet shoe.

"Rachel, one of the shoes is missing,"
she said with a frown.

"It must be somewhere around here,"
Rachel replied. "Let's look."

The girls searched the room but the ballet shoe was nowhere to be found. They went to tell Mr Robinson.

"The costumes were stored in the small dressing-room at the end of the corridor," he said, pointing it out. "The shoe probably got left behind in there. Actually..." he went on, thoughtfully.

DRESSING ROOM 2

"No one's using that dressing-room. Why don't you girls have it? Then you'll have a bit of space to practise the dance."

Rachel and Kirsty glanced at each other in delight. "Thank you!" they said together, and hurried off down the corridor carrying their costumes.

When Kirsty opened the door of
the dressing-room, it was dark inside.
Rachel felt for the light switch,
and flicked it on. Instantly, a mirror
surrounded by light bulbs filled
the room with a dazzling white light.

But a second later, one of the bulbs
popped loudly and went out. The noise
made Rachel and Kirsty jump.

"Rachel, look!" Kirsty gasped.

Sparkling gold fairy dust had burst from the broken bulb in a glittering spray. As the dust cleared, Rachel and Kirsty saw a pretty little fairy dancing in the air in front of them!

"Hello," the fairy called. "I'm Paige the Pantomime Fairy!"

"Hello, Paige" the
girls replied, staring
at the tiny fairy
who wore a short
ballet dress of
pink net sparkling
with diamond dust,
a gold tiara and dark
pink ballet shoes with tiny bows.
Quickly, Rachel shut the dressing-room
door. Meanwhile, Paige pointed her
wand at the broken bulb
and a second
later it was
shining as brightly
as the others again.
"I'm so glad to see
you, girls," Paige cried.

"It's my job to make sure that all
the Christmas shows are fun and
exciting, so that everyone has a merry
Christmas." She crossed her arms
looking very determined. "But I need
your help because Jack Frost is up
to his old tricks again," she went
on, frowning. "He wants to ruin
Christmas – for *everybody*!"

Pantomime Problem

Kirsty and Rachel gasped with dismay.

"But why?" Rachel asked.

"Because he didn't get the part he wanted in the Fairyland Christmas Show!" Paige replied, landing lightly on Rachel's shoulder. "Jack Frost wanted to be Prince Charming. Instead he got the part of Second Tree in the forest scene."

"What has he done?" Rachel asked anxiously.

Paige looked glum. "There are three special, magic shoes which help me to do my job," she explained, "and Jack Frost has sent his goblins to steal them! If they succeed, all the magic which makes the Christmas shows special will vanish!"

"What do the magic shoes look like?" Kirsty wanted to know.

"One is a ballet shoe,"
Paige replied. "It makes
sure that all the
costumes fit properly.
The second is a horseshoe,
which makes sure the props work and

the changes of scene
go smoothly. And
the last one is
Cinderella's glass
slipper. That ensures
that everyone remembers their lines."

Kirsty and Rachel
looked at each
other in dismay.

"So our show
might be a disaster,
because of Jack Frost!" cried Rachel.

Paige nodded
and flew over to
Kirsty. "One of
your ballet shoes
is missing, isn't
it?" she asked.
"Yes," Kirsty agreed.
"That's because it's not just any
old shoe," Paige went on. "It's the
magical shoe that makes everyone's
costumes fit properly."

"Mr Robinson told us
that nobody's outfits
were the right size,"
Rachel gasped.
"That must be
because the magic
ballet shoe is missing!"

"I must find that shoe," Paige said, biting her lip anxiously. "Or all the boys and girls who get taken to Christmas shows for a special treat will be so disappointed!"

"We'll help you, Paige," Rachel promised. "Won't we, Kirsty?"

Kirsty nodded. "Of course we will," she agreed.

Paige smiled and flew up into the air to do a little twirl, skirts flying. "Thank you, girls!" she cried.  "I knew you wouldn't let me down!"

"Where shall we start?" asked Kirsty. But before Rachel or Paige could reply, the dressing-room door opened very slowly and Paige zoomed to hide on Rachel's shoulder.

A moment later, the knobbly green head of a goblin appeared round the

door. Rachel and Kirsty could hardly
believe their eyes when they saw
that he had a pink satin ballet shoe
clutched in his hand!

After that Goblin!

The goblin was obviously looking for a place to hide. He almost jumped out of his skin when he saw Rachel and Kirsty. Scowling, he shoved the ballet shoe clumsily behind his back. Then he left the room, slamming the door shut and running off down the corridor.

"That goblin had my magic ballet slipper!" Paige gasped. "After him!"

The girls ran after the goblin, Paige clinging to Rachel's shoulder. They followed the sound of running footsteps into the area behind the stage. The stagehands were preparing the props for the rehearsal. Luckily they were too busy to take any notice of the girls.

"Where did the goblin go?" Kirsty wondered.

"There are three different directions
he could have taken," Rachel said
anxiously. "How will we find him now?"

"He must be here somewhere," Paige
whispered in Rachel's ear.

Just then, two stagehands passed by,
carrying a marble column for the
ballroom scene.

"I didn't think there were any goblins
in Cinderella, did you?" one
of the stagehands said to the other.

"No," his friend agreed, "but that was a really fantastic costume. It was so ugly!" Rachel and Kirsty glanced at each other. "They've seen the goblin!" Rachel gasped. "And they came from over there," Kirsty added, pointing.

The girls dashed off in the direction the stagehands had come from, and soon they came to an area where large props from previous shows were stored. It was quite dark and shadowy, but the girls could make out statues, trees, bushes and big tubs of paint, as well as doors, tables, chairs and other pieces of furniture.

"The goblin could be hiding anywhere here," Paige said, fluttering around to examine the props. "We'll have to keep our eyes open."

Rachel and Kirsty began to search for the goblin. They looked behind trees and statues and under tables and chairs, but he was nowhere to be seen.

"What now?" Kirsty
asked gloomily.

Rachel was just
about to reply when
she caught a glimpse
of something moving
out of the corner of her

eye. She spun round and saw a group
of statues. As she stared at them, one
of them moved!

Rachel nudged Kirsty. "That statue
moved!" she whispered,
pointing at it.

"And it's got
a really long nose,"
Kirsty whispered
back. "I bet
it's the goblin!"

As the girls and Paige began to creep towards him, the goblin realised he'd been spotted. With a shriek, he ran to the back of the props room.

The girls gave chase and saw the goblin make straight for the ladder leading to the catwalk, high overhead. The goblin clamped the ballet slipper between his teeth and began climbing up the ladder.

Rachel, Kirsty and Paige hurried over.

"Come down!" called Paige.

The goblin glared down at her but carried on climbing. The girls and Paige watched as he went higher and higher. Then, suddenly, he began to slow down. The girls saw him glance at the floor nervously. A look of panic came over his face and he clutched the sides of

the ladder as if he was
afraid he was
going to fall.
"I think the goblin
has just discovered
he's afraid of
heights!" said Rachel.
"Why don't
you come down?"
Paige coaxed.
The goblin shook his
head stubbornly.
Taking a deep breath,
he closed his eyes and
carried on climbing.
"With his eyes closed, he
won't be able to see where
he's going!" exclaimed Kirsty.

Suddenly the goblin missed a rung
of the ladder and his foot slipped.
He gave a frightened yell and the
ballet shoe fell from his mouth. As
it whirled downwards, ribbons flying,
the goblin reached out to grab it.

He missed, but lost his grip on the ladder. As Rachel darted forward and caught the ballet shoe, the goblin fell. He plunged backwards, arms flailing wildly!

It's Raining Goblins!

"Oh, no!" Kirsty cried. "We must break his fall!" She glanced round and spotted a big plastic tub of orange paint, standing next to Cinderella's pumpkin coach.

"Paige!" Kirsty yelled, pointing at the tub of paint.

Luckily, Paige understood exactly

what Kirsty meant. She waved her wand and a shower of magical golden sparkles swirled around the tub, pushing it across the floor until it was right underneath the goblin.

SPLASH!

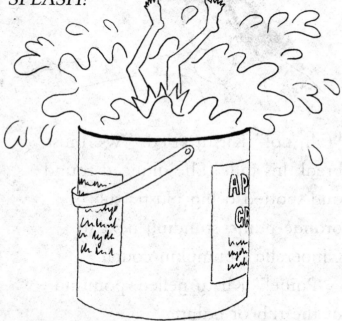

The goblin plunged into the tub.

Orange droplets of paint splattered everywhere as he sank. Then he surfaced, spluttering and wiping orange streaks from his face. "Give me that ballet shoe!" he gurgled crossly, climbing out of the tub.

"No way!" Rachel replied firmly, hiding the shoe behind her back. "It's not yours."

"Go back to Fairyland," said Kirsty, "and tell Jack Frost we're not going to let him spoil Christmas!"

Muttering angrily,
the goblin stomped
off, leaving
a trail of
orange footprints
behind him.
"I'll soon get rid of
this mess," Paige
laughed. She pointed her
wand at the footprints and soon all the
orange paint had
vanished in
a stream of sparkles.
"Thank goodness
we have the
magic ballet
shoe back," Paige
went on happily,

flying over to perch on Kirsty's shoulder. "Now your costumes will fit properly, and so will everyone else's."

"We'd better go and see Mrs Spencer, the wardrobe mistress, Kirsty," Rachel suggested. "Then the magic of the ballet shoe can get to work, and she'll be pleased that she hasn't got to alter everyone's costumes after all!"

Rachel led the way to the costume department. Then she, Kirsty and Paige peeped into the room. It was full of actors and actresses, all dressed in their show costumes. Mrs Spencer, the wardrobe mistress, was rushing here and there, a tape measure around her neck and a box of pins in her hand.

"Mrs Spencer!" Karen Lewis cried, twirling round in circles, her white dress swirling. "Look, I don't think my dress is

too long after all. In fact, it's just right!"

"And I can button my jacket now!" added the young man who was playing Prince Charming, "It felt too small a minute ago."

"Oh, thank goodness!" Mrs Spencer sighed with relief. "It looks like we all panicked too soon."

Paige beamed at the girls. "The magic of the ballet shoe is working again!" she announced joyfully.

"Let's go and change too, Kirsty," said Rachel.

Kirsty and Rachel hurried back to their dressing-room. Quickly they changed into their beautiful dresses, which fitted perfectly. Then Paige helped fix the roses in their hair.

"You look lovely!" Paige said.

Rachel and Kirsty grinned happily at each other.

"I must get back to Fairyland and tell everyone the good news," Paige went on. "Good luck with your rehearsal, girls, and I'll see you tomorrow. But don't forget, the goblins will definitely be back to cause more mischief. So keep an eye out." And, with a flick of her wand, she vanished in a mist of dazzling dust.

"Kirsty, we'd better start practising the dance steps," Rachel said. "There's a lot to learn before the show."

"And we've only got two days before opening night!" Kirsty said eagerly. "I don't want to make any mistakes. I want the show to be really good!"

"I'm sure it will be," Rachel said. "But we'll also have to stop the goblins stealing the magic horseshoe and the glass slipper. We *can't* let Jack Frost spoil our Christmas pantomime!"

More
Missing Magic

Contents

The Pantomime Ponies

The following morning the girls arrived at the theatre bright and early, ready for the final dress rehearsal. Kirsty and Rachel had been very busy practising their dance at home whenever they had a spare moment.

"We've practised so much, I think I was dancing in my sleep last night!"

Kirsty laughed. "I don't want to make any mistakes today."

"Everyone thought you did brilliantly yesterday," Rachel said. "I mean, we only had about half an hour's practice in our dressing-room before we went on stage!"

"Yes, but today we're going to be doing the whole show from start to finish," Kirsty reminded her. "That means the whole cast will be there, so I want to do it right."

"I can't wait to see Cinderella's pumpkin coach," Rachel said eagerly, as they went through the stage door.

"Alison, the actress who plays the Fairy Godmother, owns a riding stable and she's bringing two ponies to pull the coach onto the stage!"

"Oh!" Kirsty exclaimed. "Do you think one of the ponies will be wearing Paige's magic horseshoe?"

Rachel nodded solemnly. "I expect so," she replied. "We'll have to watch out for goblin tricks! If they steal the horseshoe, none of the props will work and who knows what could happen with the scenery."

"We've got to stop them," replied Kirsty. "Or horrible Jack Frost will ruin all the Christmas shows everywhere!"

As the girls were on their way to their dressing-room, they noticed a crowd of people standing in the wings. The people were gathered around two beautiful white ponies, who were harnessed to a dazzling orange and gold pumpkin coach.

"Look!" Rachel gasped. "The ponies are here."

"Let's go and see," Kirsty said eagerly. The girls hurried over to join the admiring crowd. The ponies had been carefully groomed, and their white coats gleamed. They wore pretty golden halters and glittering golden head-dresses with fluffy orange feathers.

"Aren't they lovely?" Rachel said, stroking the pony nearest to her. Both animals were very well-behaved and stood patiently as people petted them.

"They've even got golden horseshoes!" whispered Kirsty, pointing down at the ponies' sparkling hooves. "I wonder which one is the magic one." The girls tried to look more closely at the ponies' horseshoes, but it was difficult with so many other people around.

"Isn't the pumpkin coach fantastic, too?" Rachel went on. "This is going to be the best bit of the whole show!"

Suddenly the director hurried over, clutching his clipboard. "Time for you all to get changed for the dress rehearsal," he called. "The ponies are going to practise pulling the coach on and off the stage a few times before we start, so we need to clear some space."

Rachel and Kirsty gave the ponies a last pat, and dashed off to their dressing-room.

"I wonder if Paige will be waiting for us," said Kirsty as they went inside.

But there was no sign of the little fairy. Quickly the girls changed into their dresses and ballet shoes, and fixed the flowers in their hair.

"We'd better go to the make-up room now," Rachel said, once they both had their costumes on.

Very soon the two girls were ready, and it was time for the dress rehearsal to begin. Kirsty and Rachel hurried to join the rest of the cast.

"I'm really nervous," Kirsty said. "I hope I can remember everything!"

"You were wonderful yesterday, Kirsty," said Lucy, the fourth dancer in the group. "You hardly made a single mistake."

"Yes, and you'll be great today, too!" Rachel told her friend confidently.

Everyone was milling around
backstage, dressed in their costumes.
Rachel and Kirsty were thrilled to see
Cinderella in her rags, and the Ugly
Sisters in their tall powdered wigs, huge
crinoline dresses and frilly bloomers,
as well as a very smart Buttons and
a handsome Prince Charming.

"Attention everyone!" Mr Robinson
said as he bustled in. "Cinders, Buttons
and the Ugly Sisters on stage for the

first scene, please. Everyone else is to wait here until they're called." He turned to Rachel and Kirsty. "Could you two help out by carrying the Ugly Sisters' trains please?"

Rachel and Kirsty laughed as the Ugly Sisters headed towards the stage. They wore big crinoline dresses, one striped purple and yellow, the other bright pink with purple spots. Both dresses had long dragging trains.

Rachel and Kirsty picked up the Ugly Sisters' trailing skirts and helped them to take their places in the wings. Then the girls found a quiet spot where they could watch without getting in anyone's way. There was a fanfare of music, and the dress rehearsal began.

The girls really enjoyed themselves as they watched the familiar story unfolding before them. They felt sorry for Cinderella when the Ugly Sisters were rude to her and wouldn't let her go to the ball, and they wanted to cheer when the Fairy Godmother arrived in Cinderella's kitchen.

"You shall go to the ball, Cinderella!" declared the Fairy Godmother. "Bring me a pumpkin!"

Rachel nudged Kirsty and pointed at the wings opposite. The ponies were standing ready to pull the pumpkin coach on stage. As the Fairy Godmother waved her wand over the ordinary pumpkin that Cinderella brought her, there was a glittering flash of smoke. A stagehand quickly removed the pumpkin under cover of the smoke, and at the same moment another stagehand sent the ponies trotting onto the stage. The coach glittered and the ponies' white coats gleamed in the bright spotlights. Kirsty and Rachel gasped at the spectacle.

"Isn't it clever the way the pumpkin disappears and the coach takes its place?" Kirsty whispered. "It's just like real magic!"

Rachel nodded. "The audience is going to love it!" she whispered.

 But, suddenly, a piece of wooden scenery that was painted to look like a kitchen dresser laden with shelves of plates toppled over and fell to the floor with a loud *BANG!*

Everyone jumped and the ponies were startled. They whinnied with fright, and broke into a canter, dashing across the stage past Cinderella and the Fairy Godmother, and dragging the coach behind them.

"The ponies are really scared, Kirsty," Rachel cried. "We must stop them!"

Pony Problems

The ponies galloped into the wings
where Rachel and Kirsty were standing.
Quickly the two girls stepped forward
and grabbed the golden halters the
ponies were wearing, bringing them
safely to a stop.

"That wasn't supposed to happen!"
they heard Mr Robinson wail from

the front row of the theatre stalls.

"It's OK," Rachel said soothingly,
patting the pony nearest to her on the
nose. "Calm down." As she petted the
pony, she noticed a particularly
bright sparkle in
the middle of its
feathered head-dress.
Suddenly, Paige
popped out from
between the orange
feathers. "Hello, girls!"
she whispered. Then, as
Rachel heard footsteps running across
the stage towards them, Paige whizzed
over to hide on Kirsty's shoulder.

Alison, the ponies' owner, dashed up
to Kirsty and Rachel, holding up the

long skirt of her Fairy Godmother costume. "Oh, you managed to catch them!" she said gratefully. "Thanks, girls. I should have stopped them myself, but I just wasn't expecting them to bolt like that!"

"I think they're fine now," Kirsty replied, handing the halters to Alison.

"I'll just check them over," Alison said, running her hand up and down the ponies' legs. "Oh no!" she exclaimed suddenly. "Snowflake has lost one of her shoes!"

Kirsty and Rachel could see that

the golden horseshoe on Snowflake's front left hoof was missing.

"I don't understand it," Alison went on, shaking her head. "Both horses had all their shoes before the dress rehearsal!"

"Maybe Snowflake lost it on the stage," Rachel suggested.

"Or in the wings," Kirsty added.

Alison nodded. "If I can find it, my blacksmith will be able to fit it ready for the performance," she said, and hurried off.

Next moment Paige peeped out from under Kirsty's hair. "Girls, the missing horseshoe is no ordinary shoe," she announced. "It's the magic horseshoe!"

Kirsty and Rachel looked at each other in dismay.

"So that's why the piece of scenery tumbled over!" exclaimed Rachel. "Because the magic horseshoe went missing!"

Paige nodded. "I think the goblins used some of Jack Frost's magic to make the horseshoe fall off!" she explained. "Girls, we *must* get the horseshoe back!"

Horseshoe Hunting

"So there are goblins around somewhere!" said Rachel, glancing over her shoulder. "We'd better keep our eyes open."

Just then, Mr Robinson called everyone onto the stage together.

"We need to find the golden horseshoe as quickly as possible," he declared.

"Please can someone go and fetch the rest of the cast so that everyone can help look?"

Rachel and Kirsty began searching around the wings. Suddenly Rachel jumped as she heard a door slam at the top of the auditorium, near the entrance lobby of the theatre. Rachel frowned. Why would anyone leave the auditorium to search the theatre lobby? The ponies hadn't been brought in through the main entrance.

Rachel nudged Kirsty. "I think that was a goblin going into the theatre lobby," she whispered.

"Let's go and see," Paige said eagerly.

Immediately the girls left the stage and hurried up the aisle. No one took any notice because they were all intent on looking for the horseshoe. Rachel pulled the heavy door open and the two girls slipped into the lobby.

"Look!" Kirsty gasped, pointing at the stairs leading up to the balcony seats. A goblin was just disappearing round the curve in the stairs, and in his hand was a gleaming, glittering, golden horseshoe.

"We must catch him, girls!" Paige
cried. "Let me turn you into
fairies. We'll be quicker
that way."
Rachel and Kirsty
stood still as Paige
showered them with
fairy magic.
Immediately they
found themselves
shrinking until they
were exactly the same
size as the little fairy.
Glittering wings
shimmered on their backs.
The girls fluttered up into
the air and followed Paige
up the balcony staircase.

"I can't see the goblin," Rachel said anxiously as they reached the top of the stairs. "He could be hiding in the rows of seats," Kirsty pointed out. Paige and the girls flew slowly above the seats, trying to find the goblin. Suddenly Rachel spotted him. "There he is!" she whispered, pointing.

On the right-hand side of the balcony,
a goblin's head was poking up from

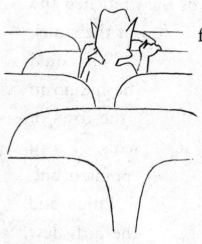

a row of seats. The
friends flew over and
hovered high above
him so he wouldn't
notice them.
They could see both
his hands and it was
clear that he didn't
have the horseshoe.

"He must have hidden it somewhere,"
Paige declared.

"But look over there," Kirsty said
pointing at the back row of seats
on the left-hand side of the balcony.
"There's another goblin!"

Sure enough, another green head was

peeking over the seats. Paige, Kirsty and Rachel rushed over, but to their dismay, that goblin didn't have the horseshoe either.

"Oh, dear!" Paige sighed. "How many goblins *are* there?"

"And which one has the horseshoe?" Rachel added.

Goblin Behind the Glass

"Let's split up and each search a section of the balcony," Kirsty suggested.

"Good idea," Paige agreed.

Rachel flew over to the right of the balcony, Kirsty to the left and Paige took the middle. Kirsty flew along the rows, but she couldn't see any more goblins. Then, Kirsty caught sight of

a burst of golden sparkles
coming from Paige's
wand in the middle of
the central row of seats.
Paige was doing a little
dance in the air, and
pointing down below her.
Paige has found the magic horseshoe!
Kirsty realised excitedly.

Rachel had noticed too. Both girls
zoomed over to Paige, who could
hardly contain her excitement. Her face
pink, she pointed her wand down at
a goblin crouched in the
middle row. There, in his
knobbly green hand,
glittered the magic
golden horseshoe.

But just at that moment the goblin glanced up. He gave a loud shriek when he saw Paige and the girls and immediately scrambled away. He ran to the end of the row, then dashed up the aisle and into a small booth at the back of the balcony.

"Where's he going?" Kirsty asked as they flew after him.

"That's the sound and light booth," Rachel explained. "It's where the engineer controls all the microphones and spotlights and special effects."

The goblin had slammed the door of the booth shut behind him, so the girls flew to the front and looked in through the large window. Hovering at the glass, Paige and the girls were dismayed to see that the goblin had used a chair to wedge the door shut.

"There's no way we can get in, not even if Paige makes us human-sized again!" Kirsty pointed out. "How are we going to get the horseshoe?"

The goblin inside the
booth was looking very
pleased with himself.
"Yah boo!" He stuck
out his tongue and
flapped his hands behind
his ears. "Can't catch me!"

The other two goblins who were
still on the balcony also started
laughing smugly.

"Not so clever now with your fairy
magic, are you?" one of them sneered.

"We've got the
magic horseshoe
and we're
not giving
it back!"
the other jeered.

But Rachel had spotted something in the wall of the booth. "Look at this air vent," she said, pointing at it. "The holes are big enough for a fairy to get through."

"You're right. Follow me," Paige called, and she flew through the air vent into the booth. Rachel and Kirsty did the same. Once inside, Paige sent a stream of sparkles over to Kirsty and Rachel, making them human-sized once more.

The goblin inside the booth was staring out of the window, apparently wondering where Paige and the girls had gone. A look of horror crossed his face when he turned and saw the girls inside the booth with him.

"Go away!" he yelled, hugging the horseshoe tightly. "You're not having it! Help!" he shrieked, backing away from the girls.

The two goblins outside dashed to the door and began rattling the door handle. But they couldn't get in.

"Give us the horseshoe, please," said Kirsty as she and Rachel moved towards the goblin.

The goblin shook his head furiously. He had now backed right up against the counter which controlled the lights. As the girls drew closer, he jumped up onto it and glared at them.

Rachel tried to grab the horseshoe but the goblin danced away out of her reach. As he did so, his big green feet pressed several of the switches.

"Hey! What's going on up there?" a loud voice demanded.

"That's Mr Robinson!" Rachel gasped. She turned to look out of the window

and saw that some of the lights on the stage were flashing on and off. The director was staring up at the balcony looking very annoyed.

"We must hurry and get the horseshoe back," Rachel told Kirsty urgently, "before Mr Robinson sends someone up here to check the lights!"

Perfect Ponies

The goblins outside on the balcony
were still trying to push their way in.
But the goblin inside the booth was
now determined to get out. He jumped
down from the control panel, dodged
past Rachel and Kirsty and dragged the
chair away from the door.

Immediately, the door burst open and

the two goblins hurtled inside. They
bumped straight into their startled friend
and the horseshoe was knocked out
of his hand. It flew across the booth.
As the goblins crashed to the floor in
a tangled heap, the magic horseshoe
landed right at Kirsty's feet.

"Thank you!" Kirsty beamed,
picking it up.

Paige fluttered over to the door.
Rachel and Kirsty followed, laughing
as they stepped over the heap of
groaning goblins.

"You'd better hurry up and leave,"
said Rachel to the goblins.

"Or we'll put make-up and dresses on
you and make you part of the show!"
Kirsty added with a grin.

The goblins scowled. Muttering and moaning, they picked themselves up as the girls left the booth.

Kirsty and Rachel hurried down the balcony stairs with Paige flying alongside. "Thank you a million times, girls!" Paige cried as they reached the lobby. "I must go back to Fairyland right away and tell everyone that the magic horseshoe is safe!" She smiled at Rachel and Kirsty. "And I'll ask India the Moonstone Fairy to send you sweet dreams so that you sleep well tonight, girls. After all, tomorrow is the grand performance of your pantomime! Goodbye!" And with a kiss and a wave, she disappeared in a shower of fairy magic.

Rachel and Kirsty hurried back into the auditorium and down the aisle towards the stage. Most of the cast and the stage crew were gathered there.

"We've looked everywhere," Cinderella was saying, "and we simply can't find the horseshoe."

"Mr Robinson!" Kirsty called, as they approached. "Rachel and I have found it!" And she held up the glittering horseshoe.

Alison rushed forward, looking very relieved. "Thank you, girls," she said gratefully, taking the horseshoe from them.

Mr Robinson clapped his hands. "Wonderful! Now we can get back to work. Let's take it from the pumpkin coach scene."

Rachel and Kirsty hurried into the wings to watch as the rehearsal began again. This time the ponies performed beautifully. They waited patiently as Cinderella, now wearing a beautiful ballgown and her glass slippers, climbed into the coach.

Then, at a signal from the Fairy
Godmother, they trotted off into the
wings where a stagehand was waiting
to grab their halters.

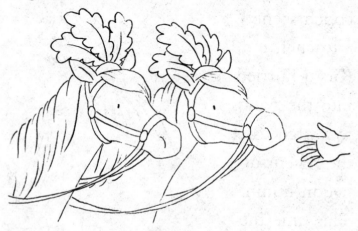

"Brilliant!" Rachel exclaimed, as she
and Kirsty gave the ponies a pat.

"The magic of the horseshoe is
making sure all the props work and no
scenery falls over!" Kirsty whispered
happily. "Now I've got to make sure

that I don't fall over when we rehearse our dance."

"You'll be great," Rachel said with a grin. "We've just got to make sure that the goblins don't get up to any more sneaky tricks before the performance tomorrow night!"

The Show Must Go On

Contents

A Cracking Surprise

"I'm nervous!" Kirsty declared as she and Rachel joined the rest of the cast backstage. "I can't believe it's the show tonight. Two days ago, I wasn't even in it!"

"No one would guess that," Rachel laughed. "You didn't make a single mistake in yesterday's dress rehearsal!"

It was Christmas Eve, and the cast of Cinderella had gathered backstage before the show.

"Well, this is it, everyone," Mr Robinson said. "Yesterday's rehearsal was fantastic, and I'm sure you'll be even better tonight with the audience cheering you on!"

Everyone clapped.

"We want the pantomime to be

fun and festive," Mr Robinson
went on. "So don't be afraid
to improvise by adding any
funny little bits of your own here
and there. And now we have
something to get you all into
the Christmas spirit..."

A stagehand stepped forward
holding a box full of crackers.
Everyone gathered round to take one.

"It's a shame my mum and dad couldn't get tickets," said Rachel, selecting a silver cracker.

Kirsty took a gold one. "I know," she agreed. "I would have liked my mum and dad to come too, but it's going to be an exciting night anyway."

"Good luck, everyone!" called Mr Robinson, as they hurried off to their dressing-rooms.

As soon as they'd closed the door, Rachel held out her cracker. "Let's see what's inside," she said with a grin.

Kirsty took the other end and pulled.

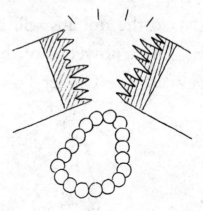

The cracker snapped
with a bang and
a pretty pearl
bracelet fell out.

"Now pull mine,"
Kirsty said, holding
out her cracker.

Rachel tugged the other end, the
cracker snapped with a burst of golden
sparkles, and Paige
zoomed out
from inside!
"It's me again,
girls!" she
announced. "Jack
Frost will be
determined to spoil
the pantomime tonight,

so the goblins will be after the
most powerful of the three magic
shoes – Cinderella's glass slipper!"

"That makes sure everyone remembers
their lines, doesn't it?" asked Kirsty.

Paige nodded. "Think how awful it
would be if nobody could remember

what to say!" she replied. "Girls, we must make sure that Jack Frost and his goblins don't get their hands on that glass slipper!"

Not the Right Lines

"Let's go and check on the glass slippers before we get changed," Rachel said.

Paige hid in Rachel's pocket and the girls ran to the props room. Cinderella's ballgown was hanging there, and next to it was a shoebox. Kirsty lifted the lid, and she, Rachel and Paige all sighed with relief as they

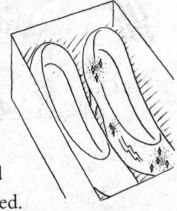

saw both glass slippers nestled inside.

"Can you tell which one is magic?"
Paige asked.

Kirsty stared at the
shoes and noticed
that one seemed to
gleam with
a rainbow-coloured
shimmer. She pointed
to it and Paige nodded.

"Yes, that's the magical one," Paige
confirmed. "Please look after it, girls."

"The stagehands put the dress and the
shoes in the wings before the show
starts," Rachel explained as they hurried
back to the dressing-room. "Luckily,
Kirsty and I come on for our dance
from the same side of the stage."

"So we'll wait there and keep
an eye on the shoes the whole time,"
Kirsty promised.

"I haven't seen any goblins so far,"
Paige said as she helped Kirsty and
Rachel into their costumes.

Rachel jumped as a bell
sounded overhead.
"That means it's
only fifteen minutes
to curtain up!"
she gasped.

"We'd better get
our make-up done,"
said Kirsty, looking nervous.

"I'll meet you in the wings," Paige
smiled at them. "Good luck. I know
you're going to be great!"

133

Ten minutes later, Kirsty and Rachel were ready. As they hurried to the wings, they could hear a loud buzz of anticipation coming from the audience out in front.

"There are the glass slippers," Kirsty said, pointing at the props which had

been placed neatly in the wings. "Hello, girls," Paige whispered, fluttering over to join them. "I've been guarding the slippers and I haven't seen a single goblin!"

"We're just in time," Rachel said as the opening music sounded. "The show is about to start."

She and Kirsty watched as the Ugly Sisters pranced on stage, their outrageous costumes making the audience roar with laughter. The girls glanced at each other in delight. The show was off to a great start.

As the moment for the shoes to go on stage came closer, the girls began to feel nervous.

"They're the last thing to go on stage after the pumpkin coach and the ballgown," Rachel whispered to Kirsty.

Back on stage, the Ugly Sisters
had left for the palace, and
Cinderella was all alone.
"I wish I could go to
the ball!" she sighed.
At that
moment, the
Fairy Godmother
sailed onto the
stage. She wore
a swirling, silver
dress and a wig
of golden curls with
a silver tiara on top.
"I am your Fairy
Godmother and you shall
go to the ball!" she declared,
raising her wand. "You shall wear

beautiful glass slippers to dance the
night away," she added, turning
to the wings. "Bring me
the glass slippers!"
Rachel and Kirsty stared
at each other, puzzled.
"I thought the
pumpkin coach
was first," Kirsty
murmured to Rachel.
Cinderella was also
looking bewildered.
"Not the shoes!"
she whispered.
"The pumpkin!"
The Fairy Godmother
scowled. "Very well," she said
sulkily. "Bring me a pumpkin!"

Cinderella did so. The girls watched as one of the crew then set off a smoke bomb so that the pumpkin could be removed from the stage. Under cover of the smoke, the ponies trotted on pulling the beautiful pumpkin coach. There was a huge burst of applause from the audience.

"Now for the glass slippers!" cried the Fairy Godmother before the audience had even finished clapping.

Rachel and Kirsty could see that Cinderella was getting annoyed.

"No, the ballgown!" they heard her whisper crossly.

"This is odd," Rachel said. "Alison never gets her lines wrong."

"Well, the goblins don't have the magic slipper," Paige said, pointing at the glass shoes waiting in the wings. "So that isn't the reason Alison's forgetting her lines!"

"Her voice is a bit gruff," Kirsty
added. "Maybe she's getting a cold."

"And now for your ballgown,
Cinderella!" shouted the Fairy
Godmother. There was another puff
of smoke and
a stagehand passed
the dress to her
so that she could
help Cinderella
put it on. There
was a gasp of
delight from the
audience as the
smoke cleared and
they saw the sparkling

ballgown for the first time.

"And now for the glass slippers!" the

Fairy Godmother said loudly, stalking closer to the wings where Kirsty and Rachel were standing.

Kirsty peered at her. Something strange seemed to be hanging from the Fairy Godmother's chin. She looked more closely and saw that it was an icicle!

"Rachel!" Kirsty whispered. "That's not the Fairy Godmother. It's Jack Frost!"

Flying Shoes

"It can't be!" Rachel exclaimed.

"It is!" Paige gasped, staring. "But how has he made himself as tall as Alison, the real Fairy Godmother?"

Paige and the girls knew that there was a rule in Fairyland that prevented anyone using magic to make themselves taller than the highest tower of the

Fairyland palace. But they didn't have time to think about that now; Jack Frost was waving the Fairy Godmother's

wand, his eyes gleaming as he stared at the glass slippers in the wings. As the stagehand set off the smoke bomb, Jack Frost reached eagerly for the slippers. As the Fairy Godmother, he was supposed to hand them to Cinderella, but Rachel and Kirsty knew that he would just run off with them.

"Oh, no, you don't!" Kirsty
murmured, snatching the glass slippers
out of Jack Frost's reach.

"Give me those slippers
IMMEDIATELY!" Jack Frost roared.

The audience began to chuckle,
thinking that this was part of the show.

As the bewildered stagehand set off
another smoke bomb, Jack Frost leaned
over and tried to grab the slippers from
Kirsty. Quickly she
handed them to
Rachel who
backed away
from Jack Frost's
icy fingers.
"What shall we
do now?" asked
Rachel, clutching
the slippers.

The smoke cleared again and the
audience laughed loudly as Jack Frost
jumped up and down with rage. "For
the last time, GIVE ME THOSE
GLASS SLIPPERS!" he howled.

"We have to get the slippers to Cinderella somehow, or we'll be ruining the show!" Kirsty said urgently. "But how can we make sure Cinders gets them and not Jack Frost?"

"Like this," Paige whispered. And as the stagehand set off yet another smoke bomb, Paige waved her wand and a stream of sparkles lifted the glass slippers from Rachel's grasp, and carried them across the stage, past Jack Frost and into the arms of a very surprised Cinderella.

The audience clapped and laughed heartily, clearly having a wonderful time.

But Jack Frost glared at Kirsty and Rachel as Cinderella put the slippers on and climbed into the pumpkin coach.

"Have a good time at the ball!" he snapped coldly to Cinderella. "But be home by midnight – or else!" Then he stomped off into the wings on the opposite side of the stage from the girls.

"Well, the magic glass slipper is safe so far," Rachel said anxiously, as the ponies pulled the coach offstage too. "But Jack Frost will be waiting for another chance to steal it!"

If the Shoe Fits...

"It's nearly time for our dance," Kirsty whispered.

Onstage, Cinderella had arrived at the ball, and was having her first romantic waltz with the prince.

"Paige, can you keep an eye out for Jack Frost and the goblins while we're performing?" asked Rachel.

Paige nodded.
"If I'm high up,
I'll be able to
see everything,"
she whispered,
zooming up to hide
among the spotlights.

Karen and Lucy hurried over to join
Rachel and Kirsty. As the waltz music
finished, the prince
led Cinderella
to a golden
chair where
she sat down,
arranging her
skirt so that
her glass slippers
were on show.

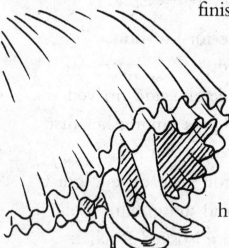

"We're on," Rachel whispered as the music for their dance began. "Good luck, everybody."

Rachel skipped lightly out of the wings, leading the girls to the centre of the stage. Kirsty took her place between Rachel and Karen. She was desperate to get the steps right, but she couldn't help wondering what Jack Frost and his goblins were up to!

Concentrate, she told herself.

The music began. And before she
knew it, Kirsty had performed the whole
dance without making a single mistake!

BONG! BONG! BONG! Right on
cue, the clock began to chime midnight.
Kirsty and Rachel
watched as
Cinderella
jumped from
her chair and
ran up the
stairs at the
back of the
stage, leaving
the magic glass
slipper on the third step.
It glittered like a diamond under
the bright white spotlights.

Immediately a small child dressed in a furry grey mouse costume darted over and grabbed the slipper, just as the prince strode forward to pick it up.

"Who's that? There isn't supposed to be a mouse!" Rachel whispered to Kirsty.

"I bet it's a goblin!" Kirsty gasped, and, sure enough, when the girls looked closely, they could see a green face behind the mouse mask!

Meanwhile, the prince was trying to wrestle the slipper from the mouse's grasp. "Hey, I'm supposed to have that!" he muttered crossly as the audience howled with laughter.

After a moment or two, the prince managed to wrench the slipper away and hold it up. "I promise I will find the owner of this glass slipper – and marry her!" he declared, as the mouse slunk furiously offstage.

The audience applauded. The curtain came down. And everyone hurried into the wings as the stagehands quickly began to change the scenery, ready for the final scene.

"Thank goodness the prince didn't let that goblin get away with the slipper!" Paige whispered, landing on Kirsty's shoulder as the curtain rose again.

The girls watched as the prince and his servants arrived at Cinderella's house with the glass slipper.
The first Ugly Sister tried the shoe on, but it didn't fit. Prince Charming shook his head and moved on to the other sister.

"Why does the second Ugly Sister look so much meaner than usual?" Rachel asked. Then she clapped a hand to her mouth. "It's Jack Frost in the Ugly Sister's costume!" she exclaimed.

"We must stop the prince giving him the slipper!" Kirsty said anxiously.

But it was too late. The prince was

down on one knee, trying to fit the
slipper onto the Ugly Sister's foot.
Rachel and Kirsty could see that
the foot was big, green and knobbly.
It was a goblin's foot!

"So that's how Jack Frost is
making himself so tall," Rachel
whispered. "He's standing on
a goblin's shoulders!"

The audience thought that the big green foot was a good joke. They roared with laughter, although the prince looked a little bewildered as he tried out the slipper. "This slipper doesn't fit," he announced, shaking his head.

"It does fit!" Jack Frost snapped. "Give it to me. I'll show you!" And he grabbed the slipper from the prince and jumped up to hurry offstage.

Immediately the prince blocked his way. "Give that back!" he demanded.

"Shan't!" Jack Frost sneered, and the audience chuckled as Kirsty, Rachel and Paige watched in dismay from the wings.

"Footmen!" the prince called desperately. "Come! Help me!"

"The prince is calling for his servants," Paige whispered, waving her wand so that Kirsty and Rachel were suddenly wearing smart red uniforms with gold buttons.  "That's you, girls!" she finished.

Quickly, Rachel and Kirsty ran onto the stage.

"We're here, Your Highness!" Kirsty announced.

The girls and the prince surrounded Jack Frost. Seeing that he had nowhere to go, Jack Frost threw the glass slipper sulkily at the prince who caught it. Grinning at each other, Rachel and Kirsty stepped to the side of the stage as Cinderella came to try on the slipper.

"It fits!" the prince announced to loud cheers from the audience. "Will you marry me, Cinderella?"

"I will," Cinderella replied, "and we'll live happily ever after!"

The prince and Cinderella began to walk off into the wings as the audience applauded. But Kirsty noticed that Jack Frost was following them.

Thinking quickly, she stepped forward. "That Ugly Sister won't leave Cinderella alone!" she called to the audience. "Can we all be very loud and warn Cinders?"

"Look out behind you, Cinderella!" shouted a little girl in the front row. Cinderella stopped and looked round. Jack Frost immediately put his hands in his pockets and whistled a tune, trying to look innocent.

Cinderella and the prince walked on, but Jack Frost sneaked after them again.

"Look out behind you, Cinderella!" Kirsty and Rachel shouted, and the audience joined in.

Cinderella whirled round and Jack Frost folded his arms, pretending to study the painted backdrop.

Then, just as Cinderella and her prince were about to leave the stage, Rachel saw Jack Frost pull his wand out of his pocket. "Oh, no!" she whispered. "Jack Frost is going to cast a spell!"

A Standing Ovation

Kirsty looked round desperately for inspiration, and suddenly noticed that Jack Frost and the goblin were standing on a trapdoor in the stage. Quickly, she turned to the wings, looking for Paige. She could just see a faint sparkle in the air where the little fairy was hovering. Trying to be subtle, Kirsty pointed at

Jack Frost and then down at the trapdoor, hoping Paige would understand.

Jack Frost raised his wand, but just as he started to say his spell, the trapdoor opened. Both the goblin and Jack Frost fell through the hole as the audience clapped enthusiastically, thinking it was part of the show.

"Merry Christmas, everyone!" called the prince and Cinderella together as the whole cast gathered on stage to bow and wave to the audience. The applause and cheers were deafening as the delighted audience gave the pantomime a standing ovation. Rachel and Kirsty smiled happily at each other. Despite Jack Frost and his goblins, the show had been an enormous success.

The curtain came down and the
audience began to leave. Meanwhile
the cast rushed backstage to change.
"Wasn't that fun?" Rachel cried. "We
didn't let Jack Frost spoil
our show. In fact,
it was brilliant!"
"The audience
loved it,"

Kirsty agreed.
"You were
wonderful!" Paige
told the girls,
happily. "You
stopped Jack Frost from
stealing the magic glass slipper, and
now, all over the world, children
can enjoy their Christmas shows!"

As the girls entered their dressing-room, all the lights around the dressing-table mirror began to flash, and then a vivid rainbow appeared, stretching from one side of the room to the other. As Kirsty and Rachel watched, spellbound, the King and Queen of the fairies stepped off the end of the rainbow.

"Girls, we have come to thank you in person for what you have done," Queen Titania smiled. "You have saved Christmas!"

"And we have sent Jack Frost back to Fairyland," King Oberon added. "He won't be causing any more trouble this Christmas."

"What happened to the real Fairy Godmother and Ugly Sister?" asked Kirsty anxiously.

"Jack Frost froze them so he could take their places," the Queen replied. "But don't worry, we've thawed them out!"

"They won't remember anything," the King chimed in. "Except that the show was a huge success."

There was a knock at the door.

"We must go," said Queen Titania quickly. She, Paige and the King stepped onto the end of the rainbow.

"Merry Christmas, girls, and thank you!" Paige cried, blowing kisses.

"And there's one more Christmas
surprise for you!" the King added
as the rainbow whisked them away.
"Goodbye..."

Rachel opened the door and stared
in amazement when she saw her
mum and dad standing outside
with Kirsty's parents.

"We saw the show!" Mrs Walker announced, beaming at Rachel and Kirsty.

"You were both wonderful!" Mrs Tate said.

"Well done," added Mr Walker, and Kirsty's dad nodded. All four of them looked very proud indeed.

"But the show was sold out," Kirsty said, looking puzzled. "How did you get tickets?"

"Well, it was strange," said Mr Walker with a frown. "We both had Christmas cards pushed through our doors this afternoon. The cards weren't signed, but there were tickets to the show inside them!"

"So we rushed over to Tippington, met up with Rachel's parents, and got here just before the show started!" explained Mr Tate.

"We'll wait outside while you get changed," Mrs Tate put in. Then she winked. "And wrap up warmly, girls, it's snowing outside!" she added.

"Well," Rachel laughed as she shut the door. "I think I know where those tickets came from."

"Yes, from our fairy friends!" Kirsty said with a grin. "And now we can really enjoy Christmas, knowing that Jack Frost and his horrible goblins can't spoil it for everyone!"

Win Rainbow Magic Goodies!

There are lots of Rainbow Magic fairies, and we want to know which one is your favourite! Send us a picture of her and tell us in thirty words why she is your favourite and why you like Rainbow Magic books. Each month we will put the entries into a draw and select one winner to receive a Rainbow Magic Sparkly T-shirt and Goody Bag!

Send your entry on a postcard to Rainbow Magic Competition, Orchard Books, 338 Euston Road, London NW1 3BH. Australian readers should email: childrens.books@hachette.com.au New Zealand readers should write to Rainbow Magic Competition, 4 Whetu Place, Mairangi Bay, Auckland NZ. Don't forget to include your name and address. Only one entry per child.

Good luck!

Where the magic begins...

Ruby the Red Fairy

When Rachel and Kirsty meet on a
holiday to Rainspell Island, they have
no idea such magical adventures
lie ahead...

The End of the Rainbow

"Look, Dad!" said Rachel Walker. She pointed across the blue-green sea at the rocky island ahead of them. The ferry was sailing towards it, dipping up and down on the rolling waves. "Is that Rainspell Island?" she asked.

Her dad nodded. "Yes, it is," he said, smiling. "Our holiday is about to begin!"

The waves slapped against the side of the ferry as it bobbed up and down on the water. Rachel felt her heart thump with excitement. She could see white cliffs and emerald green fields on the island. And

golden sandy beaches, with rock pools
dotted here and there.

Suddenly, a few fat raindrops
plopped down on to Rachel's head.
"Oh!" she gasped, surprised. The sun
was still shining.

Rachel's mum grabbed her hand.
"Let's get under cover," she said,
leading Rachel inside.

"Isn't that strange?" Rachel said.
"Sunshine *and* rain!"

"Let's hope the rain stops before we
get off the ferry," said Mr Walker.
"Now, where did I put that map of
the island?"

Rachel looked out of the window.
Her eyes opened wide.

A girl was standing alone on the
deck. Her dark hair was wet with

raindrops, but she didn't seem to care. She just stared up at the sky.

Rachel looked over at her mum and dad. They were busy studying the map. So Rachel slipped back outside to see what was so interesting.

And there it was.

In the blue sky, high above them, was the most amazing rainbow that Rachel had ever seen. One end of the rainbow was far out to sea. The other seemed to fall somewhere on Rainspell Island. All of the colours were bright and clear.

"Isn't it perfect?" the dark-haired girl whispered to Rachel.

"Yes, it is," Rachel agreed. "Are you going to Rainspell on holiday?"

The girl nodded. "We're staying for a

week," she said. "I'm Kirsty Tate."

Rachel smiled, as the rain began to
stop. "I'm Rachel Walker. We're staying
at Mermaid Cottage," she added.

"And we're at Dolphin Cottage," said
Kirsty. "Do you think we might be
near each other?"

"I hope so," Rachel replied. She had
a feeling she was going to like Kirsty.

Kirsty leaned over the rail and looked
down into the shimmering water. "The
sea looks really deep, doesn't it?" she
said. "There might even be mermaids
down there, watching us right now!"

Rachel stared at the waves. She saw
something that made her heart skip a
beat. "Look!" she said. "Is that a
mermaid's hair?" Then she laughed,
when she saw that it was just seaweed.

"It could be a mermaid's necklace," said Kirsty, smiling. "Maybe she lost it when she was trying to escape from a sea monster."

The ferry was now sailing into Rainspell's tiny harbour. Seagulls flew around them, and fishing boats bobbed on the water.

"Look at that big white cliff over there," Kirsty said. She pointed it out to Rachel. "It looks a bit like a giant's face, doesn't it?"

Rachel looked, and nodded. Kirsty seemed to see magic *everywhere*.

"There you are, Rachel!" called Mrs Walker. Rachel turned round and saw her mum and dad coming out on to the deck.

"We'll be getting off the ferry in a few minutes,"
Mrs Walker added.

"Mum, Dad, this is Kirsty," Rachel said. "She's staying at Dolphin Cottage."

"That's right next door to ours," said Mr Walker. "I remember seeing it on the map."

Rachel and Kirsty looked at each other in delight.

"I'd better go and find *my* mum and dad," said Kirsty. She looked round. "Oh, here they are."

Kirsty's mum and dad came over to say hello to the Walkers. Then the ferry docked, and everyone began to leave the boat.

"Our cottages are on the other side of the harbour," said Rachel's dad, looking at the map. "It's not far."

Mermaid Cottage and Dolphin Cottage were right next to the beach. Rachel loved her bedroom, which was high up, in the attic. From the window, she could see the waves rolling onto the sand.

A shout from outside made her look down. It was Kirsty. She was standing under the window, waving at her.

"Let's go and explore the beach!" Kirsty called.

Rachel dashed outside to join her.

Seaweed lay in piles on the sand, and there were tiny pink and white shells dotted about.

"I love it here already!" Rachel shouted happily above the noise of the seagulls.

"Me too," Kirsty said.
She pointed up at the sky. "Look, the
rainbow's still there."

Rachel looked up. The rainbow
glowed brightly among the fluffy
white clouds.

"Have you heard the story about the
pot of gold at the end of the rainbow?"
Kirsty asked.

Rachel nodded. "Yes, but that's just in
fairy stories," she said.

Kirsty grinned. "Maybe. But let's go
and find out for ourselves!"

"OK," Rachel agreed. "We can
explore the island at the same time."

They rushed back to tell their parents
where they were going. Then Kirsty
and Rachel set off along a lane behind
the cottages. It led them away from the

beach, across green fields, and towards
a small wood.

Rachel kept looking up at the
rainbow. She was worried that it would
start to fade now that the rain had
stopped. But the colours stayed clear
and bright.

"It looks like the end of the rainbow
is over there," Kirsty said. "Come on!"
And she hurried towards the trees.

The wood was cool and green after
the heat of the sun. Rachel and Kirsty
followed a winding path until they
came to a clearing. Then they both
stopped and stared.

The rainbow shone down on to the
grass through a gap in the trees.

And there, at the rainbow's end, lay
an old, black pot...

RUBY THE RED FAIRY
978-1-84362-016-7

AMBER THE ORANGE FAIRY
978-1-84362-017-4

SAFFRON THE YELLOW FAIRY
978-1-84362-018-1

FERN THE GREEN FAIRY
978-1-84362-019-8

SKY THE BLUE FAIRY
978-1-84362-020-4

IZZY THE INDIGO FAIRY
978-1-84362-021-1

HEATHER THE VIOLET FAIRY
978-1-84362-022-8

Have you checked out the

Website at:

www.rainbowmagic.co.uk

There are games, activities and
fun things to do, as well as news
and information about Rainbow
Magic and all of the fairies.